Rachel's Gift

RICHARD UNGAR

Tundra Books

Published in Canada by Tundra Books,
481 University Avenue, Toronto, Ontario M5G 2E9

Published in the United States by Tundra Books of Northern New York,
P.O. Box 1030, Plattsburgh, New York 12901

Library of Congress Control Number: 2002112168

National Library of Canada Cataloguing in Publication

Ungar, Richard
Rachel's gift / Richard Ungar.

For ages 7-10.
ISBN 0-88776-616-1

1. Chelm (Chelm, Poland) – Folklore. 2. Jews – Folklore.
I. Title.

PS8591.N42R33 2003   jC813'.6   C2002-904277-1
                            PZ7

We acknowledge the support of the Canada Council for the Arts and the
Ontario Arts Council for our publishing program.

We acknowledge the financial support of the Government of Canada through the Book Publishing
Industry Development Program for our publishing activities.

This book was inspired by the story "The Magician" by I.L. Peretz (1851–1915).

Design: Blaine Herrmann

Medium: watercolor and colored pencil on paper

Printed in Hong Kong, China

1 2 3 4 5 6   08 07 06 05 04 03

For Dayna

The people of Chelm loved the springtime. With the arrival of spring, the streets came alive with the hustle and bustle of the villagers going here and there, doing this and that, and talking about everyone and everything.

Springtime in Chelm also meant getting ready for Passover. Houses were swept from top to bottom, windows were washed until they sparkled, and all the furniture was carried outside and scrubbed clean.

"Make sure it's nice and shiny," Selma the Cook called over to her daughter, Rachel, who sat by the window polishing a spoon with a special cloth.

As she watched Rachel, Selma's lips curled in a smile. Selma knew that Passover was the time when Elijah the Prophet was rumored to be wandering the world, bestowing good fortune on the deserving. And she was determined that this very night, the first night of Passover, Elijah would pay a visit to the tiny house that she shared with her husband, Simon, and daughter, Rachel.

Just as Selma was pondering how she could entice Elijah to come to their house, there was a knock at the door.

"Special mail for Selma the Cook from the Bubbie of Bialystok," announced the messenger, who stood on the step.

Clutching the letter tightly, Selma approached Rachel, who was busy arranging some sticks in a vase. Rachel was pretending that the sticks were really roses. She loved roses because the feel of their soft petals and their sweet scent always filled her with happiness. But it was still too early in the springtime for roses to be growing, and so Rachel had to make do with sticks.

"Rachel, you have sharp eyes," said Selma. "What does this letter from my aunt say?"

Rachel held up the letter and began to read:

Dear Selma, I am finally retiring from the soup-making business. And, as my favorite niece (all right, so I don't have any other nieces), I am ready to share my secret recipe for Bubbie's Own Matzo Ball Soup.

When Selma heard this part, she exclaimed, "Simon, Rachel, we are going to be rich! Surely when Elijah tastes some of the Bubbie's Own Matzo Ball Soup, he will love it and reward us handsomely!"

Simon, too, could barely contain his excitement. Immediately, he set about preparing an extra place for Elijah at the Seder table and, as was traditional, he filled Elijah's wine cup to the brim.

"Go on, Rachel, read the recipe now," urged Selma.

Rachel continued reading aloud:

Secret Recipe for Bubbie's Own Matzo Ball Soup

A couple of chickens
Just enough onions
The right amount of carrots
Boiling water

A healthy portion of chopped-up celery, parsnips, and parsley
A pinch or two of salt and pepper
Matzo balls – made the usual way

"All right. Very good, Rachel. Now read me the rest."

"I did, Mama . . . I just read everything."

"What do you mean? Whoever heard of such a thing? A recipe that is not a recipe? Matzo balls made the usual way? Whatever does that mean?"

Grumbling, Selma set about gathering the ingredients for the soup.

"I have only two onions, so they will have to be *just enough*," she muttered, as she placed them on the small table next to the soup pot. "And I have only two carrots, so they will have to be *the right amount*," she continued.

Selma reached up to the top shelf and handed Rachel the soup bowls. Then she hunted down the other ingredients and began preparing the soup.

After a while, the fragrant aroma of matzo ball soup filled the small house.

"What do you think, Rachel? Another pinch of salt, perhaps? You know, sometimes the right little something can make a world of difference!"

But before Rachel could answer, there was a knock at the door. They looked at each other expectantly. *Could it be*?

Simon rushed to open the door for Elijah. Smiling, he flung the door open. But as soon as he saw who stood there, the smile froze on his face.

"Oy! Sarah the Weaver?"

Sarah breezed by Simon and joined Selma at the stove.

Dropping a spoon into the huge pot, she murmured, "*Mmmmm.
Not bad, Selma. And the matzo balls are nice and fluffy. But this
soup is missing a little something . . . Yes. I know. It needs some
more pepper! Where do you keep it?*"

But before Selma had a chance to answer, Myriam the
Matchmaker appeared suddenly at her side.

"Listen, Selma, I was walking by and sniffed something that
could only come from heaven. And, as your door was open,
I invited myself in. Now, don't be offended if I tell you that your
wonderful smelling soup is missing a little something. I don't
think you added enough parsley. May I?" Myriam spied some
sprigs of parsley and began chopping.

"And a Happy Passover to you and yours," said Rafael the Musician, standing in the doorway. Selma looked up and said, "Yes, yes, and the same to you, Rafael. Now, if you will kindly move away from the door . . . we are expecting an important visitor."

"Do you mean . . . ?"

"Yes, I am making this soup for Elijah."

"Then there is not much time, my friends!" exclaimed Rafael, as he strode in and joined the others by the stove. "Selma, keep stirring! Rachel, watch and do as I do. We are in luck! Your windows face west. Elijah always comes from the west. Hurry, we must blow the smell of the soup out the window."

Rafael filled his lungs and blew. Rachel did the same. Tendrils of steam from the soup wafted out the open window.

Just then, there was a knock at the door.

"Rachel, why don't you see who it is!" shouted Simon.

Rachel opened the door. The man who stood there wore patched clothes and had a wild beard that pointed in every direction.

"Good evening to you, Samuel," Rachel greeted the herring vendor. "Are you here to help with the soup?"

Samuel smiled and said, "Oh, no, Rachel. I am on my way home for the Seder. But I am weary and in need of a moment's rest."

"Certainly. Please come in."

Samuel pulled off his boots. Then he sat down and closed his eyes.

Rachel glanced at Samuel's boots. They were soaked. She picked them up and discovered that there were big holes in the soles. Quickly, she carried the boots up the short ladder to her bedroom, reached into her mattress, and grabbed two handfuls of straw. Rachel stuffed some into each boot and plugged up the holes as best she could. Then she climbed back down the ladder and placed the boots in the same spot where Samuel had left them.

A short time later, Samuel stood up and retrieved his boots. As he pulled them on, he noticed how wonderfully smooth and snug they felt.

Just before he headed out the door, Samuel paused, turned toward Rachel, and said, "Rachel, your kindness will be remembered." And then he vanished into the night.

"Where is that Elijah already?" said Selma impatiently.
"How could he resist my delicious soup? If anything,
I have improved the Bubbie's recipe!"

"Selma, my treasure, he may not have resisted it after all."

"What do you mean, Simon?"

"Look!"

Simon lifted Elijah's cup. There was no question. The level
of wine had definitely gone down.

"Father, do you think that . . . ?"

"Yes, Rachel. Elijah is the master of disguises."

After Selma had searched frantically around the house, she said, "And what about a gift for us? Did the prophet not leave us a gift?" But there were only matzos in the cupboard, dishes and glasses on the shelves, and well-worn clothes in the chest of drawers. Selma could not find Elijah's gift anywhere.

"Everyone, look!" exclaimed Rachel.

On the Seder table, there were no longer any sticks in Rachel's vase. Instead there stood a single rose, in full bloom.

Selma groaned. "What can one do with a flower? It is hardly anything!"

"But, Mama," said Rachel, smiling. "It is just as you said: sometimes the right little something can make a world of difference."